AESOP'S FOX

RETOLD AND ILLUSTRATED BY

AKI SOGABE

BROWNDEER PRESS

HARCOURT BRACE & COMPANY

San Diego   New York   London

Requests for permission to make copies of any part of the work
should be mailed to: Permissions Department, Harcourt Brace & Company,
6277 Sea Harbor Drive, Orlando, Florida 32887-6777.

Browndeer Press is a registered trademark of Harcourt Brace & Company.

Library of Congress Cataloging-in-Publication Data
Sogabe, Aki.
Aesop's fox/retold and illustrated by Aki Sogabe.
p. cm.
"Browndeer Press."
Summary: Several fables from Aesop are adapted and woven
into a story about the adventures of a fox.
ISBN 0-15-201671-6
[1. Fables. 2. Folklore.] I. Aesop's fables. II. Title.
PZ8.2.S57Aes 1999
398.24'52
[E]—dc21   97-5869

First edition
A C E F D B
Printed in Hong Kong

Each picture in this book was made from paper, cut freehand.
The color was applied using airbrush or watercolor.
The display type was set in OptiEastman.
The text type was set in Weiss.
Color separations by Bright Arts Ltd., Hong Kong
Printed by South China Printing Company, Ltd., Hong Kong
This book was printed on totally chlorine-free Nymolla Matte Art paper.
Production supervision by Stanley Redfern and Ginger Boyer
Designed by Lisa Peters

To Aesop, who told these stories first,

with thanks

One summer morning Fox woke up and started out on his search for breakfast. He couldn't find anything to eat in the forest, so

he trotted over to the nearby farmyard and saw Rooster perched on the fence post.

"Good morning, Mr. Rooster," Fox said in his most friendly manner. "I didn't hear your beautiful voice this morning. Is anything wrong? My day doesn't start without your singing."

Rooster proudly shook his crest.

"I used to listen to your uncle's song," Fox continued. "Oh, he was a great singer. And so beautiful! I miss his voice very much."

Rooster waved his elegant crest from left to right and back again.

What a vain fellow! Fox thought.

"Can you sing as well as your uncle?" Fox asked.

"Of course I can. I sing much better," Rooster finally answered proudly. He opened his beak and took a deep breath.

"Wait!" said Fox. "When your dear uncle sang, he shut his eyes very tight and stretched his neck very straight. Then he sang his heart out."

"I can certainly do that," said Rooster. He shut his eyes very tight and stretched his neck very straight. "*Cock-a-doodle-doo! Cock-a-doodle-doo!*"

Fox leaped at him, seized him by the throat, and ran toward the forest.

The farmer saw Fox and began to chase him. "Stop! Thief!" he cried, and came closer and closer.

"My dear Fox," Rooster said as Fox held him tightly in his jaws. "Why don't you just tell him that I belong to you?"

What a good idea, Fox thought. He opened his mouth and called to the farmer, "This is my rooster! My breakfast!"

At that instant Rooster flew up to a tree branch.

The hungry fox said to himself, trotting away, "Think before you speak."

As Fox walked along he heard some strange rasping sounds, and in a few moments he saw a large boar sharpening his tusks on the trunk of a tree.

Zuuuk, zuuuk, zuuuk.

"I beg your pardon," said Fox. "Why are you doing that?"

"I'm sharpening my tusks," Boar replied. "These are the only weapons I have to fight my enemies. Unlike you, I have no sharp claws or fast feet."

Fox looked about. Except for the noise Boar made, the forest was silent and peaceful. Surely this boar was a fool to spend his time this way when there was no need.

"But there's no danger here that I can see," Fox said.

"Not at this moment," replied Boar. "But when the hunters come after me with their dogs, then it will be too late to sharpen my tusks." He went back to the tree. *Zuuuk, zuuuk, zuuuk.*

Fox walked away and thought, He's right. If you are prepared to defend yourself, you have nothing to fear.

Fox was very hungry now. He soon came upon a large vineyard at the edge of the forest. Bunches of juicy grapes hung from a trellis. They looked ripe and ready to eat. They smelled delicious.

"What beautiful grapes!" Fox licked his lips and jumped up to get a bite of the purple bunches. But he couldn't reach them. He jumped again and again—and again—but the grapes remained beyond his reach. He could get nothing.

Finally he turned away and said angrily, "I didn't want those grapes anyway. Look at them! They are probably sour."

He walked back into the forest. Boar, who had been watching, said, "We often pretend to dislike what we can't have."

It was lunchtime now, and Fox was still without food.

Then Fox saw Crow sitting on a branch with a piece of cheese in her beak.

Surely this is my chance to have something to eat! he thought. And so he addressed Crow.

"What a handsome bird you are," Fox said. "Your glossy feathers are remarkable. Why, I believe not even the peacock's splendor can equal yours."

Crow seemed interested but still held the cheese tightly in her beak.

"Your noble face and bright eyes are like Eagle's—No! Not even Eagle's. If you can sing like the nightingale," Fox continued, "I will tell all the beasts that you are Queen of the Birds."

Crow had listened closely and liked what she heard. This fox told the truth. She *was* handsome and her voice *was* beautiful. She opened her beak and sang, *"Caw! Caw!"*

The piece of cheese fell into Fox's mouth. Fox gobbled it up and said to Crow, "Never believe flattery."

Fox needed a drink of water. He noticed Leopard sitting by the stream, looking at his reflection.

"Good morning, Mr. Fox," Leopard said. "I have been admiring my beauty. Don't you agree that I have the most attractive fur?"

Fox stopped and looked.

"I have the finest skin of any animal in the forest." He licked his spots to make himself more smooth. "Look at my gorgeous whiskers and my graceful walk. You know, of course, with what speed I run when I choose to do so. Every creature in the forest greatly admires me," Leopard continued, "and that is because I am simply the best. When my cousin Lion dies, I will be king." He held his nose in the air.

"You may be the most beautiful creature in this forest and perhaps you are the fastest, but you don't have a brain," Fox replied. "If you did you would know how foolish it is to boast about such things."

Fox thought, All creatures know of *my* cunning. Yet I don't have to brag about it. Before Leopard could say a word, Fox added, "The best don't need to boast." Then he vanished into the meadow.

Fox remembered he needed to visit Old Lion, who was sick and had asked him to call. Everyone knew that Lion had stayed in his cave for weeks. Many of the animals in the forest had gone to pay their respects. But not Fox. Lion sent him a message again, to say this would be the last day Fox could visit his old dying king.

"Greetings, great lord," said Fox, standing outside Lion's cave.

Old Lion lay in dark shadows. "Oh, my dear, dear friend, Mr. Fox," he said in a weak voice. "Why don't you come closer so I can see you?" He coughed. "I've been so ill I can hardly move."

"Closer?" said Fox. "No thank you. I see many footprints going into your cave but none coming out."

Fox ran farther into the woods and said to himself, "Better safe than sorry."

After taking a nap Fox trotted down the path and saw Rabbit

huddled in the underbrush, trembling. A few seconds later Deer ran

past him with terror in her eyes. Fox became alarmed. Obviously some
terrible danger lurked in the forest.

Peering over a hedge, he was surprised to see Old Lion snarling and pawing the ground. But when Fox looked more closely, he saw it wasn't Lion at all—it was Donkey. He was draped in a lion's skin and was enjoying the spectacle of the forest animals who ran in fear at the sight of him.

Fox leaped over the hedge and stood in front of Donkey.

"So you aren't afraid of the King of Beasts," Donkey said to Fox in a

growly voice. "We'll see about that!" He bared his teeth and gave his best imitation of Lion's roar.

"Hee-haw! Hee-haw!"

Fox burst out laughing. "You can't frighten me," he said. "I see your gray ears under the lion's skin and I hear your bray." He trotted through the forest thinking, No matter how hard you try, you can't hide your true self.

It was late and Fox was getting hungry again. He sniffed the air for something good to eat, and this time his nose took him to a small hollow in a big oak tree. Inside he saw some fragrant bread and fruit that had been left by a woodcutter a short time earlier. Fox crept inside the hollow and ate every last morsel.

"That was delicious," said Fox. "I am finally satisfied. Time to go." But when he tried to crawl out of the hollow, he found he was stuck. He had

eaten so much that his stomach was too big to squeeze through the narrow space. To make matters worse, his meal had made him very thirsty. "I can't even get a drink of water," cried Fox. "What shall I do?"

Raccoon passed by and heard Fox's lament. "You'll have to stay there until your stomach shrinks again," he said wisely. "Next time don't be so greedy."

Fox had to admit Raccoon was right. He settled back into the hollow.

"Ah, well," he said. "Time fixes everything."

Fox fell fast asleep.

And by the time the moon rose, Farmer, Rooster, Boar,

Crow, Leopard, Lion, Rabbit, Deer, Donkey,

and Raccoon had done the same.